The Couples Would You Rather Edition

+

Truth Or Dare

Beckie Reid

The Couples Would You Rather Edition

Beckie Reid

How To Play ...

1) Have two or more people around (the more the better).

2) The person holding the book asks the question and the person listening HAS to answer one of the two options (no skipping).

3) Take turns asking questions (Don't keep the book to yourself).

4) That's it, have fun!

In case you didn't know ...

Angels Three-way : A guy with two women in bed.

Devil's Three-way : Two guys with one women in bed.

Ex : A former girlfriend, boyfriend, husband or wife.

Golden Shower : Peeing on someone for sexual desire.

Hall Pass: When your partner gives you permission to see other people.

Hickie: A bruise on someone's skin from being bitten, kissed or sucked too hard.

Nymph (Nymphomaniac) : A woman with uncontrollable or excessive sexual desire.

PDA (Public Display of Affection) - Can be holding hands, hugging, kissing or groping without sex of any kind in public.

1

Would You Rather...

Get to fall asleep next to your partner and not wake up with them because they work early

or

Get to wake up with them but not cuddle them to sleep because they work late?

2

Would You Rather...

Ask ten randoms on the street if you can give them oral

or

Ask one person who you work with if they'd give you oral?

3

Would You Rather...

Have sex with an erotica audio book on in the background

or

Have sex with porn on in the background?

4

Would You Rather...

Be with someone who uses too much tongue when they make out

or

Someone who doesn't use any tongue?

5

Would You Rather...

Get your partner off under the table at a family dinner

or

Rub them off in a crowded and busy restaurant?

6

Would You Rather...

Sleep with your boss at work for three months to get a raise

or

Sleep with three different people at work to get a promotion?

7

Would You Rather...

Cry when you orgasm

or

Accidentally poop a little every time you finish?

8

Would You Rather...

Rather have a naked picture of yourself surface the internet

or

Have a video of you having sex play on live television for a few seconds?

9

Would You Rather...

Have group sex with all of your exes

or

With a bunch of randoms you've never met before?

10

Would You Rather...

Be caught naked at school/work once in front of everyone

or

Walked in by your partner's parents masturbating once?

11

Would You Rather...

Be in bed with someone who asks too many questions

or

With someone who apologizes a lot?

12

Would You Rather...

Get oral sex in a public place if there was no chance of getting caught

or

Give oral sex in a public place?

13

Would You Rather...

Someone who shows a lot of PDA

or

Shows no PDA at all?

14

Would You Rather...

Accidentally upload nudes to your family's whatsapp group

or

Accidentally post a nude on Instagram and not realise for a few minutes?

15

Would You Rather...

Sniff your best friend's underwear

or

Wear your best friend's used underwear for a day?

16

Would You Rather...

Everyone thinks that your partner worked in the porn industry

or

That everyone thinks your mum was a stripper?

17

Would You Rather...

Accidentally send a nude to your boss

or

Accidentally send it to your mum?

18

Would You Rather...

Have sex when you're on MDMA

or

When you're drunk?

19

Would You Rather...

Have your ass eaten out

or

Eat out your partner's ass?

20

Would You Rather...

Your partner be more rough in bed

or

Be more gentle?

21

Would You Rather...

That your partner work at a strip joint

or

That your partner is the Madam at a brothel?

22

Would You Rather...

Not be able to shower for an entire month after a day of rough sex

or

Have no sex for the whole year?

23

Would You Rather...

Play with ice on your partner's body

or

Hot wax from a candle?

24

Would You Rather...

Do it in the changing rooms of a department store

or

Do it in the toilets of an aeroplane?

25

Would You Rather...

Discover your partner slept with their ex

or

Slept with one of your friends?

26

Would You Rather...

Have a porn star who's great at sex as a partner

or

Have a stripper who doesn't sleep with anyone as your partner?

27

Would You Rather...

Someone in bed who doesn't like giving head

or

Someone who only wants to have anal sex all the time?

28

Would You Rather...

Only be able to receive oral ever again

or

Only be able to give it?

29

Would You Rather...

Not be able to have another orgasm for a year

or

Have an orgasm every few minutes for a month?

30

Would You Rather...

Big boobs on a person

or

A big ass?

31

Would You Rather...

Give up making out with your partner for the rest of your life

or

Give up any foreplay before sex?

32

Would You Rather...

Use the pull out method, never catch anything but potentially get a woman pregnant

or

Always use protection, even with all your long-term partner's?

33

Would You Rather...

Have your parents sit on the couch getting semen on themselves but not know what it is

or

Have your parents see a bunch of used condoms and a dildo in your bathroom?

34

Would You Rather...

See your partner sleep with your best friend

or

See them sleep with your worst enemy?

35

Would You Rather...

Another girl in bed with you

or

Another guy?

36

Would You Rather...

Come home after a few drinks and only have sex once and no sex in the morning

or

Come home hammered, no sex at night but get to lie in bed and have sex all morning/day?

37

Would You Rather...

Be really bad at foreplay

or

Be really bad at sex?

38

Would You Rather...

Walk in on your partner's parents

or

Your partner's parents walk in on you?

39

Would You Rather...

Someone with massive muscles like a bodybuilder who's super inflexible in bed

or

Someone with a scrawny marathon runner body who can last for hours?

40

Would You Rather...

Get paid to have sex from an unattractive person

or

Pay to sleep with your perfect ten?

41

Would You Rather...

Have gentle and romantic sex for the rest of your life

or

Have rough and wild sex forever?

42

Would You Rather...

Finger/be fingered in an eight bed mixed dorm room

or

On a park bench in a quiet park?

43

Would You Rather...

Have a partner who's better looking than you

or

Worse looking than you?

44

Would You Rather...

An attractive person who's bad in bed

or

An unattractive person who's really good in bed?

45

Would You Rather...

Do it in the back seat of the car like the old days

or

In the back row of the movie cinemas?

46

Would You Rather...

Be in a relationship with someone to later find out they are your cousin

or

Never find out that you're related?

47

Would You Rather...

Have a really flexible partner that can do all sorts of crazy moves in bed

or

Be the flexible one yourself so you can do the crazy moves?

48

Would You Rather...

Have a partner put a screwdriver up your bum with the metal end

or

Have them insert it with the plastic end?

49

Would You Rather...

Someone who can't make you cum at all

or

Someone who does but also cums very quickly themselves?

50

Would You Rather...

A scratcher and biter in bed

or

A screamer in bed?

51

Would You Rather...

Your partner cum on your face

or

Pee on your face?

52

Would You Rather...

Relax and get a hot, steamy, oil massage

or

Tie your partner up and be able to do what you want to them for twenty minutes?

53

Would You Rather...

Rather be a good dancer and know how to strip tease to turn on your partner

or

Have your partner be a good dancer/strip teaser so you can watch and enjoy?

54

Would You Rather...

Masturbate and have your partner watch you

or

Watch your partner masturbate?

55

Would You Rather...

Get to have a model in bed for a night

or

Someone you'll have the best sex ever with?

56

Would You Rather...

Do it when it's three degrees celsius

or

When it's thirty degrees celsius ?

57

Would You Rather...

Watch a stranger have sex with a sheep

or

Watch a stranger get a horse off?

58

Would You Rather...

Hear that you're a bad at giving head

or

Bad at sex?

59

Would You Rather...

Have sex with someone whose just exercised and is sweaty

or

Someone who has just taken a dump and still smells from it?

60

Would You Rather...

Have a really weird and disturbing face when you cum

or

Make a horrific sound when you finish?

61

Would You Rather...

Choose an outfit for your partner they have to wear

or

Dress up yourself and surprise your partner to see the look on their face?

62

Would You Rather...

Have someone in bed who's got an amazing body with toned muscles but bad at sex

or

Someone great at sex but has an average body with a big beer belly?

63

Would You Rather...

Be on top while having sex for the rest of your life

or

Be on the bottom for the rest of your life?

64

Would You Rather...

Lose your virginity to another virgin

or

Lose it to someone who was really good?

65

Would You Rather...

Hear no noise throughout all of the sex until the orgasm

or

Hear a lot of noise and nothing for the orgasm?

66

Would You Rather...

Be with a virgin

or

Or with a sex addict?

67

Would You Rather...

Have sex in a jacuzzi and swap with the hot couple next to you

or

Have sex in a hotel pool while a crowd of people watch from the windows in the building next door?

68

Would You Rather...

Listen to your grandpa talk about all the women he slept with when he was younger for an hour

or

Listen to your grandma read aloud erotica for five minutes?

69

Would You Rather...

Watch your partner make out with a random person for five minutes straight

or

Listen to them have sex with a random stranger in another room for a minute?

70

Would You Rather...

Be able to get horny on command

or

Be able to cum on command?

71

Would You Rather...

Watch porn in a room full of strangers

or

Get drunk at a party and do a striptease in front of all your friends?

The Couples Truth Or Dare Edition

Beckie Reid

How To Play ...

1) The person holding the book asks the question and the person listening HAS to answer *either* the Truth or the Dare (no skipping). You can answer both if you life.

2) Take turns asking questions (Don't keep the book to yourself).

3) Don't forget to ask why your partner chose that!

4) That's it, have fun!

1

Truth or Dare?

TRUTH: How many times a week do you touch yourself?

or

DARE: Go online and order your partner a sex toy you think they'd like.

2

Truth or Dare?

TRUTH: What's the most number of times you've cum in one day?

or

DARE: Be a slave to your partner. Do whatever they tell you to do.

3

Truth or Dare?

TRUTH: What did you want to do to me the first time you saw me?

or

DARE: Pull up your favourite porn site on your phone right now.

4

Truth or Dare?

TRUTH: How many partners have you had?

or

DARE: Send a nude to your ex.

5

Truth or Dare?

TRUTH: Do you like telling me what to do in bed, or do you prefer to be told what to do?

or

DARE: Look at your partner's eyes while you rub two fingers up and down your tongue.

6

Truth or Dare?

TRUTH: Have you ever done it while other people were around without them knowing?

or

DARE: Put a hickey on the inner thigh of your partner.

7

Truth or Dare?

TRUTH: Who is the most inappropriate person you've had a sexual fantasy about?

or

DARE: Pull your partner's hair slowly with your hand on his/her breasts.

8

Truth or Dare?

TRUTH: Have you ever lied to your partner to avoid an intimate moment, for example, say that you feel sick?

or

DARE: Take your partner into the closet or somewhere dark and make out in there.

9

Truth or Dare?

TRUTH: If you could suddenly become invisible, what more naughty things would you do?

or

DARE: Yell out the first word that comes to your mind right now.

10

Truth or Dare?

TRUTH: What's the filthiest thing you've imagined doing to me?

or

DARE: Suck your partner's nipples for sixty seconds while you stare them in the eyes.

11

Truth or Dare?

TRUTH: Have you ever paid for sex?

or

DARE: Stream your favorite porn for the next 2 minutes.

12

Truth or Dare?

TRUTH: How old do you think is too old for someone to still be a virgin?

or

DARE: Do an impression of your partner in bed.

13

Truth or Dare?

TRUTH: What's the least amount of time that's passed between you having sex with two different people?

or

DARE: Give a back rub to your partner for two minutes.

14

Truth or Dare?

TRUTH: What is the worst sexual experience you've ever had?

or

DARE: Moan and Groan like you are about to cum.

15

Truth or Dare?

TRUTH: Where do you see us going?

or

DARE: Try not to get turned on while your partner sits on your lap and kiss your earlobe for sixty seconds.

16

Truth or Dare?

TRUTH: Have you ever thought about me in the shower?

or

DARE: Try to turn me on using touch, but you can only touch my arms and hands.

17

Truth or Dare?

TRUTH: Would you ever watch your partner have sex with someone else?

or

DARE: Wear a finger moustache for the next three minutes.

18

Truth or Dare?

TRUTH: If you could double the amount in your bank account or double the amount of sexual partners you've had, which would you pick?

or

DARE: Whisper in my ear a sexy nickname you've never called me but always wanted to try.

19

Truth or Dare?

TRUTH: What fictional character do you fantasize about?

or

DARE: Pretend you are a cop who wants to arrest me for the crime of being too sexy.

20

Truth or Dare?

TRUTH: Would you rather dominate someone or be dominated?

or

DARE: Act like you are about to have an orgasm.

21

Truth or Dare?

TRUTH: Have you ever taken it in the butt or would you?

or

DARE: Grab both your partners breast and squeeze them as hard as you can until they tell you to stop.

22

Truth or Dare?

TRUTH: What's your secret talent in bed?

or

DARE: Kiss and lick my lips and try to get me to lose control and kiss you.

23

Truth or Dare?

TRUTH: Who is your favorite porn star?

or

DARE: Yell out the first word that comes to your mind right now.

24

Truth or Dare?

TRUTH: If you could have one sexual superpower, what would it be?

or

DARE: Recite a line from Romeo and Juliet in stripper voice.

25

Truth or Dare?

TRUTH: Where is the strangest place you've ever had sex?

or

DARE: Close your eyes for a minute and let the other person do what ever they like to you. You can't move!

26

Truth or Dare?

TRUTH: What's the most public place you'd have sex with someone?

or

DARE: Nibble on your partner's ear lobes for thirty seconds.

27

Truth or Dare?

TRUTH: Have you ever called someone else (or been called) 'Daddy'?

or

DARE: Do twenty pushups.

28

Truth or Dare?

TRUTH: Do you have a milf?

or

DARE: Eat the closest thing to you as seductively as possible.

29

Truth or Dare?

TRUTH: What is the longest you've ever given head?

or

DARE: Do a sexy dance for your partner, but you can only use one leg.

30

Truth or Dare?

TRUTH: How often do you watch something naughty?

or

DARE: Call up someone ten years younger/older and talk dirty to them for a minute.

31

Truth or Dare?

TRUTH: How many people have you kissed?

or

DARE: Bite/kiss your partner's booty.

32

Truth or Dare?

TRUTH: Do you prefer to have music in the background, or for it to be quiet?

or

DARE: Make up a short rap about your partner.

33

Truth or Dare?

TRUTH: Has anyone ever caught you having sex?

or

DARE: Get within one inch of the partner, look them straight in the eye, and tell them how you feel about them for one minute. Do not touch them.

34

Truth or Dare?

TRUTH: Is sex better when you're in love, or better when the partner is hot and mysterious?

or

DARE: Bite your partners lips until they say to stop.

35

Truth or Dare?

TRUTH: What is your favorite position?

or

DARE: Spank your partner in the most erotic way you can.

36

Truth or Dare?

TRUTH: Who was your first partner?

or

DARE: Send me the dirtiest text you can think of to the last person you texted.

37

Truth or Dare?

TRUTH: What is the most effort you've gone to to have sex?

or

DARE: Only use sign language for the next two minutes.

38

Truth or Dare?

TRUTH: What's the least sexy thing anyone's ever said to you (while trying to be sexy)?

or

DARE: Suck your partner's tongue like a straw.

39

Truth or Dare?

TRUTH: What is the dumbest thing you've said to your partner during intimacy?

or

DARE: Use your finger to brush your partner's teeth.

40

Truth or Dare?

TRUTH: What is your favorite type of porn?

or

DARE: Take a selfie with the toilet and send it to your ex.

41

Truth or Dare?

TRUTH: Have you ever cheated on your partner and if you did, why?

or

DARE: Belly dance to a country song.

42

Truth or Dare?

TRUTH: What's the least amount of time you've known someone before you've had sex with them?

or

DARE: Send a Facebook message to someone you've slept with describing a dirty dream you've had about them.

43

Truth or Dare?

TRUTH: What is your strangest sexual fantasy?

or

DARE: Imagine yourself having anal sex while asleep and react.

44

Truth or Dare?

TRUTH: Do you like a lot of foreplay? What kind?

or

DARE: Sing everything you say for the next five minutes.

45

Truth or Dare?

TRUTH: If you had to fuck one animal, what animal would you pick?

or

DARE: Make eye contact with your partner as you pretend you're banging them from behind for thirty seconds.

46

Truth or Dare?

TRUTH: What's #1 on your sexual bucket list right now?

or

DARE: Pound on your chest and act like a gorilla for the next minute.

47

Truth or Dare?

TRUTH: Tell an erotic story your best friend experienced last.

or

DARE: Tickle your partner for thirty seconds non-stop.

48

Truth or Dare?

TRUTH: What does it take for you to have a one-night stand?

or

DARE: Take off your pants for the rest of the game.

49

Truth or Dare?

TRUTH: If you could choose to do anything you would like to do tonight, what would it be?

or

DARE: Let your partner guess and kiss you on your favorite place.

50

Truth or Dare?

TRUTH: What's a sex act most people like that you think is overrated?

or

DARE: Show me the sexiest picture you have on your phone.

51

Truth or Dare?

TRUTH: What is the largest age gap you've had between you and someone you've had sex with?

or

DARE: Give a concert with your air guitar.

52

Truth or Dare?

TRUTH: Have you ever made a video of yourself?

or

DARE: Let your partner rub your inner thighs, but don't let yourself get hard.

53

Truth or Dare?

TRUTH: What's your biggest sexual fear?

or

DARE: Sing the chorus of a song you've had sex to.

54

Truth or Dare?

TRUTH: Have you ever wanted me to tie you up?

or

DARE: Call your mom and tell her how much you love her in a non-sexual way.

55

Truth or Dare?

TRUTH: Have you ever taken someone's virginity?

or

DARE: Spell out a secret message on your partner's back. If they get it right, they get a special favor of their choosing. If they get it wrong, they have to do something special for you.

56

Truth or Dare?

TRUTH: Do you prefer the lights on or off?

or

DARE: Dip your hands in your partner's pants and suck your fingers seductively.

57

Truth or Dare?

TRUTH: Do you have any sex tapes?

or

DARE: Put something edible on my forearm and lick it off.

58

Truth or Dare?

TRUTH: What's the least sexual thing I've done that has gotten you aroused?

or

DARE: Suck on my finger and pretend you're performing oral sex for 30 seconds.

59

Truth or Dare?

TRUTH: What do you wish someone would have told you about sex way earlier?

or

DARE: Say the alphabet backwards.

60

Truth or Dare?

TRUTH: What is a somewhat weird fetish that you would actually try?

or

DARE: Show me the dirtiest image you have on your phone.

61

Truth or Dare?

TRUTH: How do you feel about sex in groups?

or

DARE: Let me lick your lips and you have to resist kissing or touching me the whole time.

62

Truth or Dare?

TRUTH: What was your best sexual experience?

or

DARE: With your eyes closed, give head to an imaginary dick/pussy.

63

Truth or Dare?

TRUTH: What's a common fetish that you would never try in real life?

or

DARE: Whisper something in my ear that you think will turn me on.

64

Truth or Dare?

TRUTH: What sexual act arouses you the most?

or

DARE: Ride your partner with clothes on and bounce on them twenty times.

65

Truth or Dare?

TRUTH: Which of your co-players do you think is in for a visit to a swinger's club?

or

DARE: Pick up any book or magazine in the room and read from it as seductively as possible.

66

Truth or Dare?

TRUTH: Describe how your orgasm feels?

or

DARE: Give cute little pecks all around your partner's face for a minute.

67

Truth or Dare?

TRUTH: Would you rather spank someone or be spanked?

or

DARE: Blow on the back of your partner's neck, alternating hot and cool for one minute. Do not touch them.

68

Truth or Dare?

TRUTH: What is your role-playing fantasy?

or

DARE: Show me with your hands what you want my tongue to do.

69

Truth or Dare?

TRUTH: What is one thing that gets you hot and bothered every time?

or

DARE: You have to call one of your partner's parents and tell them how much you love your partner.

70

Truth or Dare?

TRUTH: What's the weirdest thing you've ever done while masturbating?

or

DARE: Sit on top of your partner for the next round.

71

Truth or Dare?

TRUTH: What's one sexual experience you would want to erase from your memory?

or

DARE: Blindfold yourself or close your eyes while your partner kisses your favorite part of your body for sixty seconds.

72

Truth or Dare?

TRUTH: How many orgasms have you had in one sexual encounter?

or

DARE: Do an Impression of your partner.

73

Truth or Dare?

TRUTH: What's the first thing you'd do if you could inhabit the body of the opposite sex for one hour?

or

DARE: Send a suggestive text message to someone in your phone.

74

Truth or Dare?

TRUTH: What one sexual experience do you think about most often?

or

DARE: Whisper in my ear something sexy about me you've fantasized about while you've made yourself cum.

75

Truth or Dare?

TRUTH: Do you know the last name of everyone you've had sex with?

or

DARE: Slowly bring your fingers up from their ankle to their inner thigh, ending by cupping your hand in-between their legs.

76

Truth or Dare?

TRUTH: Have you ever kicked someone out of your bed immediately after having sex?

or

DARE: Send a risky text to one family member.

77

Truth or Dare?

TRUTH: Does size matter?

or

DARE: Act like your favorite Disney character for a minute and see if your partner can guess who it is.

78

Truth or Dare?

TRUTH: Would you rather have sex on the first date or just a romantic kiss at the end?

or

DARE: Give your partner a foot rub for a minute.

79

Truth or Dare?

TRUTH: How many sex partners do you believe is too many?

or

DARE: Take your shirt off, twirl it in the air and then put it between your legs and ride it.

80

Truth or Dare?

TRUTH: What do you think is the sexiest body part of the opposite sex?

or

DARE: Say the funniest thing you've heard in a porno.

81

Truth or Dare?

TRUTH: Do you like a lot of foreplay?

or

DARE: Suck your partner's toes.

82

Truth or Dare?

TRUTH: What's something most people don't like in bed, but you can't get enough of?

or

DARE: Give your partner the hottest hickey on their neck.

83

Truth or Dare?

TRUTH: Do you like anal?

or

DARE: As a guy, wiggle your dick in front of your partner for 10 seconds.

84

Truth or Dare?

TRUTH: Would you ever have sex for money?

or

DARE: Call a local pizza place and try to convince someone that you need a 'special' delivery person.

85

Truth or Dare?

TRUTH: Have you ever performed oral on someone of the same sex?

or

DARE: Kiss your partner for every lie you've told today.

86

Truth or Dare?

TRUTH: What kind of porn did you last watch?

or

DARE: Go in the bathroom and take a suggestive selfie and send it to me.

87

Truth or Dare?

TRUTH: Would you rather fuck someone 20 years older or 20 years younger?

or

DARE: Take a naked selfie and send it to your partner.

88

Truth or Dare?

TRUTH: Have you ever thought of cheating on your boyfriend/girlfriend?

or

DARE: Let some saliva drop from your tongue to your hand and then put it back in your mouth.

89

Truth or Dare?

TRUTH: If you were forced to have sex with someone in your extended family, who would you pick?

or

DARE: Put your hand down your partner's pants until the next round.

90

Truth or Dare?

TRUTH: What's the biggest lie you've told in order to get someone into bed?

or

DARE: Whisper in your partner's ear what you're going to do to them tonight.

91

Truth or Dare?

TRUTH: If you had the power to give or receive unlimited orgasms, what would you pick?

or

DARE: Make a poem using your partner's name and dildo.

92

Truth or Dare?

TRUTH: Describe your worst date ever?

or

DARE: Pound on your chest and act like a gorilla for the next minute.

93

Truth or Dare?

TRUTH: If you had to choose between only oral sex or only penetrative sex for the rest of your life, which one would you pick?

or

DARE: Put a blindfold on or cover your eyes and try to guess which body part I'm touching you with.

94

Truth or Dare?

TRUTH: Have you ever had sex with more than one person at a time?

or

DARE: Do your best slut drop.

95

Truth or Dare?

TRUTH: What is your favorite part of foreplay?

or

DARE: Blow a raspberry on your partner's stomach.

96

Truth or Dare?

TRUTH: Spit or Swallow?

or

DARE: Take your partner's phone and scroll through their last few messages.

97

Truth or Dare?

TRUTH: Would you rather sleep with only insanely hot people or sleep with only people who think you're insanely hot?

or

DARE: Like a picture on Facebook of you and your ex.

98

Truth or Dare?

TRUTH: How many sexual partners have you had in the past year?

or

DARE: Jump on your partners back and get them to do a squat.

99

Truth or Dare?

TRUTH: What do you think is the sexiest body part of your same sex?

or

DARE: Pet your partner like a dog and talk to them like they're a good little puppy.

100

Truth or Dare?

TRUTH: How many times a week do you touch yourself?

or

DARE: Play a song you'd like to have sex to.

101

Truth or Dare?

TRUTH: What is the best time of day to have sex?

or

DARE: Hump the air like you're having the best sex ever for a minute straight.

102

Truth or Dare?

TRUTH: What sex act would you never do again?

or

DARE: Pretend to finger a girl as hard and fast as you can.

103

Truth or Dare?

TRUTH: What's your wildest fantasy?

or

DARE: Pretend to suck a popsicle; move it from cheek to cheek and choke on it.

104

Truth or Dare?

TRUTH: How much money would your boss has to offer you before you slept with him or her?

or

DARE: Twerk like Miley Cyrus.

105

Truth or Dare?

TRUTH: Have you ever done it at work?

or

DARE: Let your partner pat you down like they do in the airport.

106

Truth or Dare?

TRUTH: Do you prefer for your partner to be silent, or do you like moans?

or

DARE: Call an escort service and ask how much it is.

107

Truth or Dare?

TRUTH: Do you prefer to be on the top or the bottom?

or

DARE: Imitate your partner's best sex position.

108

Truth or Dare?

TRUTH: Have you ever done it while other people were around without them knowing?

or

DARE: Unzip your partner's pants using anything but your hands

109

Truth or Dare?

TRUTH: Do you like telling me what to do in bed, or do you prefer to be told what to do?

or

DARE: Pretend you're auditioning for a porno saying why you'd be good at it.

110

Truth or Dare?

TRUTH: How many partners have you had?

or

DARE: Get into your best kamasutra sex position.

111

Truth or Dare?

TRUTH: What did you want to do to me the first time you saw me?

or

DARE: Pretend to walk down the runway like you're a Victoria Secret model.

The End

www.ingramcontent.com/pod-product-compliance
Lightning Source LLC
Chambersburg PA
CBHW060610310726
48982CB00003B/513

* 9 7 8 1 9 2 5 9 9 2 6 4 9 *